Tangerine and Kiwi

Visit the Apple Orchard

For all the young apple lovers.

– Laïla

To Daniel, a proud accomplice in the
pursuit of my dreams.

– Nathalie

© 2006 Bayard Canada Books Inc.

Publisher: Jennifer Canham
Editorial Director: Mary Beth Leatherdale
Assistant Editor: David Field
Production Manager: Lesley Zimic
Production Editor: Larissa Byj
Designer: Kathy Ko
Cover Design: Stephanie Olive

English translation © Sarah Cummins from *Mandarine et Kiwi: La croustade aux pommes* published by Bayard Canada Books in 2006.

Special thanks to Jean-François Bouchard, Paule Brière, Sarah Trusty, Barb Kelly, Maria Birmingham, and Professor John Cline, Department of Plant Agriculture, University of Guelph.

We gratefully acknowledge the financial support of the government of Canada through the Book Publishing Industry Development Program (BPIDP), the Canada Council for the Arts, and the government of Quebec (SODEC) for our publishing activities.

 Conseil des Arts du Canada   Canada Council for the Arts

Library and Archives Canada Cataloguing in Publication

Héloua, Laïla
    Tangerine and Kiwi : visit the apple orchard / Laïla Héloua, Nathalie Lapierre, Sarah Cummins.

Translation of: Mandarine et Kiwi : la croustade aux pommes.
ISBN 2-89579-114-7
ISBN 978-2-89579-114-0

    I. Lapierre, Nathalie II. Cummins, Sarah III. Title.

PS8615.E46M3613 2006   jC843'.6   C2006-903298-X

Printed in Canada

Owlkids
10 Lower Spadina Ave., Suite 400
Toronto, Ontario M5V 2Z2
Ph: 416-340-2700
Fax: 416-340-9769

Owl kids

From the publisher of

chirp   chickaDEE   OWL

Visit us online!
www.owlkids.com

Tangerine and Kiwi

Visit the Apple Orchard

Story: Laïla Héloua

Illustrations: Nathalie Lapierre

Owl kids

Translation: Sarah Cummins

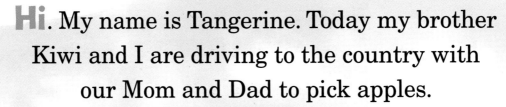

Hi. My name is Tangerine. Today my brother Kiwi and I are driving to the country with our Mom and Dad to pick apples.

"Autumn's here," says Dad. "The apples are ripe and ready to eat."

Mom asks if we know where
apples come from.

"That's easy!" says Kiwi.
"From apple trees!"

"No, Kiwi," I say. "They come
from an orchard!"

"You're both right," says Mom.
"Apples grow on apple trees,
and apple trees grow in orchards.
There are twelve different kinds
of apples at the Rosy Red
Apple Orchard!"

When we arrive at the orchard, we meet Bella, an apple grower. She gives each of us a bag to hold the apples that we pick. It's her job to look after the apple trees. She makes sure that the trees have enough water and that they aren't harmed by insects. Apple growers also trim the branches. If the trees are cared for properly, they will grow a huge crop of beautiful apples.

Bella uses a tractor and wagon to take us out to the apple trees. What a bumpy ride! But it's fun to drive through the orchard. It's like riding through a forest. There are trees to the left, trees to the right, trees everywhere.

While Dad, Mom, and I pick apples, Kiwi stops to play. He spies his pet worm up on a high branch.

"Tangerine, did you throw my worm into the tree?" Kiwi asks.

"No!" I say. "He must have climbed up there by himself."

"Your worm probably likes apples. Some worms do," explains Mom. "But no one likes to bite into an apple and find a worm! Apple growers use traps to see how many worms and bugs are in the trees. If there are too many, they might spray the trees to keep the pests away!"

With Kiwi's worm safe and sound, we get back to picking apples.

"Help, Dad!" Kiwi calls. "I can't reach that apple!"

"I'll lift you up, Kiwi. Here you go!"

With Dad's help, Kiwi picks the apple just like Bella taught us. You shouldn't tear it off the branch. Instead, you gently twist it and lift it until the stem breaks free. Then, you carefully put the apple into the bag so it won't get bruised.

Hooray, my bag is full of apples!

"Great, Tangerine!" says Mom. "I see you picked a lot of different kinds. You have McIntosh, Gala, Golden Delicious, and Spartan apples in your bag. Mmm! I think we have enough apples for our apple crisp."

"Yes, let's go home now!" cries Kiwi. "Mom, it's my turn to help make the apple crisp."

Back at home, we get to work. First, we gently wash the apples to clean any sprays and dirt off of them. Then we peel and core them.

"Kiwi, is the topping ready?" asks Mom.

"Yes, it's all ready. I have a special recipe for apple crisp. I always put chocolate on top of the apples."

I like cinnamon better, but today we are trying Kiwi's recipe.

"Mmm, your crisp is yummy, Kiwi," I say. "But next time, we'll make my recipe, right, Mom?"

Apple trees throughout the seasons

1 In winter, the apple trees are resting. The branches can be trimmed or pruned, so the tree won't be hurt by blizzards and the weight of the snow.

Winter

2 By the end of May, the smell of the apple blossoms spreads throughout the orchard. Bees gather pollen from one blossom and take it to another. This is called pollination. Once a blossom is pollinated, it can grow into an apple. Bees are so important to apple trees that some apple growers rent beehives for their orchards.

Spring

3 To grow the best quality apples, harmful insects and diseases must be controlled. If there are too many insects or if a disease is found, apple trees are sometimes sprayed with insecticides and fungicides. Often, apple growers depend on helpful insects, like ladybugs, to eat harmful bugs like aphids and mites.

Summer

4 Autumn is harvest time. Apples are a fragile fruit and must be picked by hand. Then, they are shipped to a refrigerated warehouse where they can be kept fresh. Apples can be eaten fresh, or turned into apple juice, applesauce, jelly, vinegar, or cider.

Autumn

With an adult's help, try Tangerine and Kiwi's favourite apple crisp.

Kiwi's Apple Crisp Recipe

Filling

4 or 5 medium-sized apples

8 mL (½ tbsp) lemon juice

30 mL (2 tbsp) brown sugar

60 mL (¼ cup) semi-sweet chocolate chips (for Tangerine's recipe, use 1.5 mL [¼ tsp] cinnamon instead)

Topping

80 mL (⅓ cup) flour

160 mL (⅔ cup) rolled oats

45 mL (3 tbsp) brown sugar

60 mL (¼ cup) unsalted butter, softened

Serves 4

❶ Preheat the oven to 190° C (375° F).

❷ Peel, core, and slice the apples. Toss them with lemon juice and brown sugar. Spread them in a lightly-greased baking dish. Sprinkle mixture with chocolate chips (or cinnamon). Set aside.

❸ Mix together the flour, rolled oats, and brown sugar. In a separate bowl, beat the butter until creamy. Mix the butter into the dry ingredients. Spread the mixture over the apples. Bake for 30 minutes.

❹ Apple crisp can be served warm or at room temperature. Top with vanilla ice cream.